The Berenstain Bears®

LEARN TO SHARE

Stan & Jan Berenstain

Reader's Digest **Kids**

Westport, Connecticut

I'm Sister Bear.
I'm here to say
that what I like
to do is PLAY.

I run.

I skip.

I jump.

I climb.

I have myself
a great old time!

Who's the one
I play with best,
play with better
than the rest?

Just turn the page
and you will see
my favorite playmate—

little me!

It's lots of fun
to play with me.
I ask my dolls
to come to tea.

I have my games
all to myself,
and every toy
on each big shelf.

I take each turn
on my red truck.

I do not share
my pull-toy duck.

I don't have to share
*any*thing.
It's all for me—
each and every
single thing.

But sometimes
I get tired of me,
a little *bored*
with little me.

That's when I know
it's time to share
my playthings with
my fellow bear.

One is fun,
but it is true
that many games
are best with two.

When I am sure
I need another,
I go look
for my big brother.

We play checkers,

beanbags,

pick-up-sticks.

Beating him is how
I get my kicks.

Look! Here come Liz
and Bob and Clem.
Now we can share
with *all* of them.

I ride Bob's bike.
He rides my trike.
It's great. We share
and share alike.

So, sharing's fun.
It's good to do,
and lots of times—
it's easy, too.

And if you share
it's also true
your fellow bear
will share with you!

We share our time
when we're together.
We run, we hide,
skim stones—whatever.

We share our books.

We trade our cards.

We visit one
another's yards.

Now we are more
than three or four.
We're five, six, seven,
and lots, lots more!

Here come Millie,
Mike, and Nat.
Anna May has brought
her cat.

Here comes Fred
with Snuff, his terrier!
This way, friends!
The more the merrier!

This way, cubs!
Come one! Come all!
We'll choose up sides
to play baseball.

A game of ball
is lots of fun.
We pitch. We bat.
Look! Too-Tall hit
a big home run!

It works out well
if you can share
your playthings
with your fellow bear.

The ball is mine.
It's Freddy's bat.
Lizzy brought
a glove and hat.

She'll share her hat
but not her glove.
Uh-oh! Fred gives her
a little shove.

Soon, there are lots of arguments.

Of course, I put in
my two cents!

Well, there goes the bat,
there goes the glove—
and all because
of a little shove.

But that's okay
with this small bear.
Tomorrow's another
day to share.

Meanwhile, friends,
it's still today.
And there is still
some time to play.
So turn the page.
Again you'll see …

my favorite playmate—
little me!